The True Story of Aunt Mabel's Dead Cat

Jon. Holden

(Australia)

Address all enquiries to the publisher at:

info@festoonpublishing.com.au

Copies of this book can be obtained by accessing the Festoon Publishing website: www.festoonpublishing.com.au

Book cover design by the author.

Cover graphics and illustrations by Mister Ink.

hello@misterink.com.au

A catalogue record of this book is held in the National Library of Australia.

THE TRUE STORY OF AUNT MABEL'S DEAD CAT

1st Edition: June 2024 ISBN: 978-0-6457371-2-7
2nd Edition October 2025 ISBN: 978-0-6457371-7-2

Printed by Ingram Spark

For Bonnie Jane

O wretched man that I am! Who shall deliver me from this body of death? [1]

[1] Romans 7:24 (The Holy Bible - English Majority Text Version)

CONTENTS

PREFACE

When the author was a young boy - perhaps sixty years or so ago - he remembers a story that his father told him about an elderly aunt who had a pet cat that had died and her predicament of how to give it a nice, dignified burial without her being seen to be somewhat eccentric over the matter. This book is a recollection of that story as best as the author can remember.

Unfortunately, over the years, there are many details that have long since been forgotten, like for example, the name of the aunt and the name of the cat. A check with the author's brothers' memories hasn't yielded any better clarity, but hey, why let a few details get in the way of telling a good story.

Now here's the good bit - since no one can remember much of the detail, it remains that the author can now 'embellish' the storyline without repercussions from any of his detail-minded fact-checking brothers. I will leave it to the reader to decide what parts they think to be true and what parts are a complete fabrication of events to support the story.

Please be advised that names used in this story are fictional and have no connection to people, either living or deceased, except where actual historical events are mentioned.

I hope you enjoy hearing about this true story of Aunt Mabel's Dead Cat as much as I did when it was first told to a family of young children all those many decades ago.

ACKNOWLEDGEMENTS

To my father Philip Walton Holden, who had a great sense of humour and enjoyed recounting the interesting and fun times of his childhood to his dear children of tender age.

A special thank you to my wife Sue, son Jordan, and to Robert and Sally Laurent, who have worked through the manuscript to make it more readable.

The author is deeply indebted to Gail Olrich and her cat "Puddy" for starring on the front cover of this book. Thank you for being 'Aunt Mable' for the day and getting your seventeen-and-a-half-year-old "Puddy" to cooperate for the camera for the occasion - which she did so quite admirably, (eventually)!

To Gina Franks who added the backstory to "Puddy" and to her mother, Dorothy, who adopted the stray kitten when it wandered into their front yard.

INTRODUCTION

There are some things that are simply stranger than fiction. This story recounts one of those strange events that occurred long ago but still captures the imagination of today's generation.

This book isn't so much about the historical events that happened so long ago but the coming to 'life' of the emotional and mental distresses of a poor dear old lady living in the heart of Sydney - Aunt Mabel.

There are emotional anxieties that we are so familiar with today in our everyday life – but those anxieties were just as real for previous generations that have lived long before us.

These are real people – our ancestors. We mostly identify them as being 'stiffened' characters wearing layer upon layer of old-fashioned clothing, whom we now find as images in albums of sepia-toned faded photographs. The story of Aunt Mabel comes to life as we identify with her in the dilemma that she faced with the burying of her favourite cat, - Tiddles.

Time is not on Aunt Mabel's side as this story takes place in the middle of an Australian hot summer and.... well, you can imagine what the consequences would be if Tiddles didn't get buried, and buried real soon!

This book is also a glimpse into the mind of the elderly. To younger folk the elderly can sometimes appear quite amusing in their eccentric ways, but they can be very frustrating at other times. For the elderly, everyday life can be packed with real-life drama. It seems that we are never without our cares and troubles as long as we live.

This is also a story about how God cares for His own, and in an amusing way - just like a piglet - there's a twist to the tail (tale) at the end!

Enjoy the true story about the adventures of Aunt Mabel and her precious and dearest cat – Tiddles.

"Tiddles"

Aunt Mabel

Suzanne

James & Anne Walton

Rev. Arthur Madden

Todmorden in the days when Aunt Mabel decided to leave for cleaner air in Australia.

Todmorden today - surrounded by beauty.

The cameras of the 1940's were quite simple in comparison to today's cameras. They had a simple lens at the front attached to bellows which allowed the lens to move back and forth.
This action enabled the image to focus on the negative at the back of the camera.
A lever at the front adjusted the aperture which varied the amount of light required to expose the film.

Kodak SIX-20

Sydney Ferry the "Kangaroo"

Aunt Mabel

Aunt Mabel was born in a little cottage in a lovely part of England between Yorkshire and Lancashire on the outskirts of a small English town called Todmorden. The year was 1880 and Todmorden was flourishing. It was originally a mere village with a woollen textile industry at its centre, but, with some capital input from the Fielden family and the coinciding industrial revolution, the latest technology of the time was brought to this sleepy little hamlet. Todmorden changed from a woollen manufacturing town to a cotton manufacturing one with an accompanying surge in population growth - almost doubling to 25,000 in just over a decade or so.

Aunt Mabel had fond memories of her early childhood days in her village when people had time for each other. They would stop and say "hello," chat about the weather and whatever was the talk-of-the-day. Everyone always seemed to have had a cheery disposition about life. Life was simple but made the more enjoyable by the many sociable interactions with friends and family. The factories changed all that. Time was money, and money was everything to the factory bosses. These were the city taskmasters from London that made demands rather than asking politely as had been the custom amongst the townspeople before they arrived.

The Fielden brothers who owned the local cotton gin could see how the long hours of work were adversely affecting peoples' lives and sought to remedy this by helping to secure the parliamentary 'Ten Hours Act', thus limiting the time children were allowed to work in a day. In that busy little industrial town, the Fieldens weren't just admired for what they were doing for the poor - they were loved. They became heroic figures across the nation.

Mabel was an only child of a property landlord by the name of James Walton and his wife, who was Anne Shackleton (perhaps related to Ernest Shackleton, the famous Antarctic explorer?) They were wealthy enough by their standards to not have to work too hard for a living, as James would lease out areas of his land tenure to local farmers who needed more land to generate a greater income for their desired wellbeing and comfort.

Wellbeing and comfort would mean the ability to add an additional room to a farmer's cramped cottage, or perhaps it would afford the luxury of installing a bathtub in the house rather than having to wash in a tub in the middle of the kitchen floor. Whatever the case, there was no shortage of farmers taking advantage of utilising some extra land for some additional income.

Mabel had the benefit of getting a better-than-most

education from a tutor that lived in the village – Arthur Madden, an elderly gentleman who supplemented his meagre income as a Primitive Methodist minister by teaching. (If people couldn't afford lessons, they would do work around the yard instead, like gardening or doing odd repairs to pay for it.) Besides teaching Mabel stories from the Bible, Arthur also taught her how to paint with watercolours. Mabel was an intelligent girl and quickly mastered the art of how to mix colours, how to hold the brush, and how to create different effects with the various brush strokes - but also most importantly – how to use her imagination!

An artist without imagination is like a sailor without a boat or a stockman without a horse, but an artist with imagination can create, and Mabel was definitely the creative type. She learned quickly, and before long she was selling her creative works at the local market, and it wasn't long before her works were sought after in the wealthy establishments of London, and even in Paris of all places!

There are some people who are never meant to marry, and Aunt Mabel was one of those types. Right from a very early age she was the type of girl that just loved doing things her own way, or not at all. That led to some rather feisty altercations with her parents, and with her schoolteachers in particular. She just couldn't help it – it was just the way she was, and no amount of discipline seemed to do any good – if anything it made her all the more stubborn, to the consternation of one and all!

Of course, these character traits didn't bode well for her in her teenage years when various young men would call upon her in order to get to know her better with a view to courtship. She was just as obstinate and impossible with those young men as she was with everyone else. Needless to say, she never courted with anyone seriously for any length of time and remained a spinster all of her days.

For most people, being single all their lives would be considered a rather miserable state of affairs, but not for Aunt Mabel. She rather enjoyed her own company and revelled at the thought of not letting people know what she intended doing, or where she was going. I guess that she was somewhat self-centred in that she wasn't considering the fact that other people cared about her welfare - in case something went wrong for her. For Aunt Mabel though, she would just rely upon her own resources to get herself out of trouble if and whenever it were to arise - which was more often than she knew, for the townsfolk were always averting danger before it actually occurred – for her sake and for her family's sake.

When Aunt Mabel finished her education, she was restless and wanted to move away from the now soot-ridden hometown she had grown up in and move to where the air was cleaner. She wanted to be able to smell the freshness of a new day rather than the polluted air from the many chimney stacks that crammed into her once pristine environment.

Many of Mabel's favourite memories of Todmorden were not in fact her own. She had envisioned the country landscape as if it were her mother painting a picture on the canvas of her mind, as she told of stories of long ago of the beautiful surroundings that once were - before the roads were widened to carry heavy traffic, and then of course, the railway tracks that were laid across the valleys and then went on to carve their way through the hills - primarily to aid in commerce, but also to carry well-to-do passengers to far-flung 'exotic' destinations across the British Isles.

It wasn't just the pollution that prompted Mabel to sell up and move. There were a series of events over the course of the last couple of years that weighed heavily on her once contented outlook on life. Four years earlier, both her parents had passed away within a short time of each other. They had left her with the entire estate, which she now had to learn how to manage. This she found to be a rather onerous disposition to her life of undisturbed liberties. Added to this, she kept receiving letters from a close friend who had recently immigrated to Australia.

Her friend Suzanne would write about the beautiful weather, the Australian birds, the bush animals, and the beautiful harbour on which Sydney was established. The more Suzanne wrote, the more Mabel decided that Sydney was where she was meant to be. It wasn't long before Mabel was on a ship sailing to her new homeland – Australia!

Tiddles the Cat

Aunt Mabel found herself quite at home in Australia as Suzanne would show her the sights around Sydney. On hot summer days they would often go on day-trips up to the Blue Mountains by train where the mountain air was so much cooler than in Sydney. It was there in the bush that Mabel would paint landscapes and capture on canvas the odd-looking tree that grew in Australia – the Eucalyptus or gum tree as it was commonly called. It was most intriguing to the European visitor as the Eucalyptus would shed its bark in summer, whereas trees in England and Europe tend to shed their leaves in winter.

At first, Mabel shared a room in Suzanne's parents' house in Bankstown until she got her bearings in catching transport and in finding her way around the city. She would often walk to a tram stop or the railway station as they were both within easy walking distance from Suzanne's place. She would ride to an 'unknown destination' that looked interesting, hop off, look around at the various shops and sites that it had to offer, and then return home in the afternoon. She soon got to know Sydney better than many of the locals. Aunt Mabel never did learn to drive a car.

Aunt Mabel knew that she just couldn't keep living off her inheritance without the money going dry eventually. She talked things over with Suzanne and her parents and decided that the best way forward was to learn photography and open her own studio, where she could also display and sell some of her paintings. It was an ambitious idea, but she decided to give it a go.

* * * * * * * *

In Aunt Mabel's retirement years, she would often reflect on how fortunate she was to have had such a successful career in photography with her little studio filled with paintings of what she remembered of England. Her Australian paintings were never as successful as her English paintings. She surmised that for the average Australian, the English landscape was the more beautiful with their bright evergreen foliage compared to the more pastel shades of the Australian landscape.

In the day that Mabel took up photography, photos were all black and white - or else a sepia tone was added for effect, (this was usually applied to allay the chemical effect of black and white photos fading with age - but it also had a most desirable effect of giving a portrait photograph a 'warmth' to it, that made the black and white photos appear to be harsh in contrast).

Mabel wouldn't just take a photograph – she would enhance it with an added hint of colour to the eyes and lips to give it a more life-like appearance without going so far as doing a colour fill-in on top of a photograph as was the habit of some at the time. Again, Mabel acquired quite a remarkable reputation, this time for doing family portraits, wedding photos and even on occasions, photos of a deceased person where the grieving family had no photos of the deceased to remember them with.

Aunt Mabel was so successful in her business venture that she ended up leasing a shop in Thomas Street, Chatswood. It was ideal, a short walk to the railway station and not far from the city centre of Sydney.

When she first started out with photography, she would spend hours travelling around Sydney going to weddings and posh houses with her magnificent Kodak Monitor SIX-20 camera and a box of flash bulbs to meet with her customers, but as time went by and people were more in demand of her remarkable talent, she made the move to where the people would come to her.

The added cost of renting a shop was more than offset by the additional number of customers that she could photograph in a day. These were but memories now, but her camera, she held onto that and kept it in a cardboard box on top of her wardrobe as a keepsake. The box was once the packaging for an electric frypan which was a very special treat that she bought for herself a few months earlier.

* * * * * * * *

She had long ago moved out of the upper floor of the shop that was both home and work at the one address. She was alone now with just her memories and her cat "Tiddles" who was her constant companion. Even in her old age - she was now seventy-eight - she had no regrets at having not ever married. She had her cat to talk to and she was content. She had never known the pleasure of sharing one's life with a spouse and growing old together. It may have been that she could never bear the thought of losing someone so very close to her heart. She kept her heart to herself.

Sometimes things just creep up unawares, and this was the case with Aunt Mabel and her affection towards her pet cat. Mabel had been living alone in her little cottage in Granville (just two train stops short of Paramatta) for about five years now, and she was getting it decorated into the type of house that she wanted for herself. The curtains were the first things that had to go. There was nothing wrong with them, they just lacked colour and vibrancy, (these things matter to an artist) whereas the former owners seemed to think grey curtains with dark green stripes looked wonderful - or else that was all they could afford - whatever the case, every room now looked spectacular with floral patterned curtains!

Once much of the house had been transformed and Aunt Mabel was able to work on tidying up the garden, she recalled the time when a little tabby kitten squeezed its way through a gap between the fence and the gate post and sidled up to her. Aunt Mabel wasn't too fond of cats or any other pets for that matter, so she picked the kitten up and promptly placed it outside her fence with a few parting words like; "Scat," "Go home," but no, as soon as Aunt Mabel got back to digging, that little pest of a cat reappeared beside her, this time with a little nudging of its tiny head against her knee. Aunt Mabel promptly repeated the process, and the kitten likewise repeated the process by coming back.

It was at this third time that something softened in Aunt Mabel's heart, for she picked it up tenderly, looked straight into its eyes and spoke softly to it. "Are you hungry? Would you like a drink of milk?" whereupon she dropped what she was doing and provided the poor little wretched thing a saucer of milk. She squatted down to where the kitten was greedily lapping up the milk, stroked its head with two outstretched fingers and exclaimed, "I think I'll call you 'Tiddles'" - and that marked the beginning of a very close friendship indeed.

The Cat Dies (Very Sad)

The companionship that had developed between Aunt Mabel and Tiddles was more than what most pet owners have for their pets. This relationship that Mabel had with Tiddles was something special. Aunt Mabel would often be thinking aloud and saying things like; "Shall I do the washing today or tomorrow?" at which the cat would respond with a long drawn-out "meow." Aunt Mabel would then interpret this as being an answer to her question, whereupon she would answer herself by speaking to herself with; "Yes, I think tomorrow would be better - don't you?" looking at Tiddles, and then hearing a confirmation coming as another "meow." "Well, that settles it, I'll do the washing tomorrow then" - and so the conversation would continue through the day and into the night.

It was on a warm balmy evening in her cosy little cottage that Aunt Mabel was found sitting in her favourite lounge chair, reminiscing over her years that seemed to have flown by in such a short time. She had Tiddles on her lap and a photo album on her knees, and she was slowly turning the pages in such a way as to not disturb the cat in any way.

Aunt Mabel was commenting on each photo, and as she did so, she would point her finger at each one as if the cat needed guidance in this matter. She needn't have bothered as Tiddles was not at all interested - he was purring almost as loud as Aunt Mable was speaking. Aunt Mable eventually came to the end of the album, put the cat down and made her way to the kitchen where she made herself a cup of tea before reclining to bed for the night.

The next morning, Aunt Mabel made her way into the kitchen with her empty cup and saucer and was about to put the kettle on when she noticed something odd - Tiddles wasn't making a fuss wanting his breakfast as he normally did at that time of the morning. Where was Tiddles?

It didn't take long to discover where Tiddles lay, for he was sprawled out beneath the kitchen table - quite dead!

"Tiddles, Tiddles, Oh my dearest Tiddles!" Aunt Mabel cried out with alarm in her voice. She began to sob.

"Oh! My dearest Tiddles."

Aunt Mabel had all at once experienced the overwhelming, heartfelt grief, of losing a dear friend in death that she wasn't at all prepared for. She couldn't bear to hold him, for by this stage rigor mortis had set in and Tiddles was quite stiff and cold.

It took some time before Aunt Mabel could gather her thoughts together and begin to think rationally. The first thing she thought of was that Tiddles needed a decent burial - not dropped into a rubbish bin or discarded in some other crude heartless way - but a decent burial befitting a friend with all the dignity and stateliness deserving of royalty (but within the constraints of an aged pensioner's budget.) She skipped breakfast and went straight into action...

Getting dressed gave Aunt Mabel time to think and strategise. She needed a clear head and a well-thought-out plan. She had never given a cat a dignified burial before so she couldn't just do what was the first thing that popped into her head – Oh no, a clear well-thought-out plan was what was needed.

She began to think about making a coffin. Of course, a wooden coffin was quite out of the question, it wasn't because she didn't know how to make a wooden box, it was because time was now of the essence. It would not have been long before the blowflies found Tiddles and that would have been a ghastly set of circumstances to have to deal with. It had to be a strong cardboard box that she already possessed around the house.

Now, because Tiddles had gone stiff from rigor mortis, he was now in a very awkward shape that required a much larger box than what he would normally have been able to fit into. Mabel set about trying to find just the right size box that would do the job. After trying several boxes that she was using for storage for various items around the house, she eventually settled on one that was not too big and not too small. It was a cardboard box that was on top of her wardrobe - the one that was the packaging for her electric frypan. The camera would have to find somewhere else to live.

Although Tiddles fitted into the cardboard box snugly, burying Tiddles in an electric frypan box just didn't look right – it needed to be 'prettied up' somehow. It needed some nice wrapping paper to give it some dignity. Aunt Mabel set about looking through her collection of new and used wrapping paper, but to her consternation, she couldn't find anything suitable – it was either the right pattern but too small a scrap, or it was simply the wrong pattern altogether. Mabel decided that the only paper she could use for this most solemn occasion was Christmas wrapping paper! She had it in abundance as it was the week before Christmas, and she had just recently purchased a plentiful supply.

It wasn't long before Tiddles was nicely gift-wrapped complete with ribbon and a nice crimson red bow attached. It wasn't perfect, but it was the best that Mabel could do under the circumstance. Now for the burial!

The Burial Goes Wrong

Aunt Mabel had envisioned a burial plot in her front garden amongst the beautiful flowers that she first weeded when Tiddles appeared all those years before. She thought of playing some sad requiem music composed by Mozart through the open window as she would perform the burial ceremony.

She began digging into the soft soil and she stopped after the second shovel full. She realised that she could never admire her beautiful flowers in quite the same way knowing that it was now a cemetery. She would not be able to dig in the garden again without possibly disturbing Tiddles' remains. It was then that a stray dog passed by and the thought occurred to her 'What if a dog jumped the fence and dug up Tiddles remains and started....' Ugh! The thought was too horrible to think about ... waking up one morning and seeing bits of half chewed Tiddles scattered across her front lawn. Perish the thought! No - she had a better idea! The backyard!

The backyard of Aunt Mabel's house was all lawn and had a high fence, so it would not have quite the same sentimental value as the front yard which was her little display garden. Aunt Mabel went to the back fence and began to dig, or that was what she was hoping to do. She had forgotten just how hard the ground was – it was like concrete! Aunt Mabel persevered for the best part of half an hour when she suddenly realised that at this rate, she would be there all day and half the night before she had a hole deep enough so as not to be the cause of foul odours wafting over the neighbour's fence. No, the backyard would not do, there had to be a better idea. Immediately she thought of the Council garden in the park just a couple of streets away. Yes! that would be the perfect spot for Tiddles, and she could have the beautiful memories of Tiddles every time she walked by.

It only took Aunt Mabel ten minutes or so to get all the implements together into her shopping trolley[1] and set off for the Council Park. The number of choice locations was seemingly endless. She strolled past a number of places that would have been perfect, and eventually settled upon a spot that was amongst the daffodils in bright sunlight. She immediately set to work.

She placed the brightly decorated box on the ground beside her and began to slip on a pair of gardening gloves. She was about to withdraw a small shovel from the trolley when a passer-by caught her eye. It was only then that she realised that people would be thinking that she had come to steal flowers from the garden. She couldn't proclaim her innocence by declaring to

[1] A shopping trolley was similar in size to a golf bag on wheels that women of that era did their shopping with when they didn't have a car to bring their groceries home.

all and sundry that she had only come to bury a cat – she would have looked an eccentric fool! She gradually took off her gloves and picked up the box containing Tiddles and proceeded to return home. Aunt Mabel by this stage had run out of ideas and was feeling like an old sentimental fool-of-a-lady – but she just couldn't bring herself to dump Tiddles in a rubbish bin. Aunt Mabel felt lonely, defeated and quite miserable. She didn't know what to do next.

Aunt Mabel arrived home and by this stage she was quite hungry. She hadn't eaten anything all day. She placed the precious box containing Tiddles on a chair and proceeded to make lunch while she gave the matter some more serious thought.

She was eating her last sandwich and sipping a cup of tea when she found herself looking blankly at the wall in the opposite room. When her eyes began to focus, she realised that she was staring at a picture of an old sailing ship on the high seas under full sail. "Eureka! That's it!" she exclaimed out loud. A burial at sea! How imaginative, how special that would be, she thought.

Fortified with new vigour, Aunt Mabel decided the best way to do a burial at sea was to catch the Manly Ferry from Sydney Cove, and simply toss Tiddles into the sea when the vessel was halfway across the bay. She wasted no time in getting her hat and jacket and doing the brief walk to the train station.

Aunt Mabel sat quietly on the platform trying not to be anxious. So far nothing had worked out as she had planned all day. Presently her train pulled up and interrupted her thoughts. She boarded with her 'special' parcel and was off to Circular Quay where she caught the next ferry heading towards Manly. At last, everything was going to plan, and Aunt Mabel was feeling quite at peace for the first time throughout the whole horrid muddle-of-a-day.

It wasn't long before Aunt Mabel was on the ferry and on her way to Manley. She chose a seat towards the back of the boat so that she could execute her plan without too much fuss. She placed her precious package on her lap and waited for the perfect time. It was a beautiful day and there were people standing around, just glad for the refreshing sea breeze and admiring the change of scenery as the ferry chugged its way across the harbour.

Aunt Mabel was getting more and more anxious as time went by. She had no idea when the exact time would become the 'perfect time' for Tiddles to be cast overboard, and as she hesitated, it became obvious to her that she had missed the 'perfect' opportunity altogether, as the ferry was now fast approaching the Manly jetty. Aunt Mabel scolded herself for not being decisive. "I should have acted when the opportunity first presented itself instead of waiting for the last moment."

All was not lost though, for Mabel had a return ticket and all she had to do was stay onboard and wait for the return journey to commence. The fifteen-minute wait seemed to take an eternity to come to pass, but eventually the boat was full and was making its way back to Sydney Cove. This time, Aunt Mabel was determined to carry out her plan and not be so silly about things. She was thinking about how she had wasted nearly the whole day, and here she was almost wasting the opportunity to be free of what had now become a burden to her - sending Tiddles off to his final resting place.

Aunt Mabel waited patiently and when she knew that the ferry was about halfway across the bay, she got up from her seat and made her way to the stern of the boat. She took a long last look at her precious parcel and was about to cast it overboard when she noticed some off-duty sailors in uniform standing nearby watching her. All at once, she lost her nerve.

The thought crossed her mind that one of those brave young men might think that she had accidentally dropped something valuable overboard, and leap into the water to retrieve it for her. Of course, when the parcel and sailor were safely back onboard again, there would be the insistence from all the passengers and crew that the parcel be unwrapped to make sure that the contents were still OK and not water damaged. The embarrassment would have been too much for her to bear, especially when the whole ship would find out that the sailor risked his life to save a dead cat!

Aunt Mabel returned to her seat and continued the journey back to Sydney Cove feeling quite dejected, this time there were simply no more plans left on how to dispose of Tiddles with dignity and honour.

This ought to have been the end of the story, with Aunt Mabel resorting to having to chip away in her backyard until her hands became sore and blistered. She wasn't looking forward to her journey home for every mile travelled would be shouting "DEFEAT" at her, instead, she did something that she ought to have done right from the beginning. She said a little silent prayer, (something that she would normally do except that the emotions of the day had carried her away - for she was a God-fearing believer.) She simply said, "Oh please help me Jesus, I just don't know what to do."

It was at this time that Aunt Mabel was passing through the turnstiles where she was fumbling through her handbag when a nice young man offered to hold the parcel for her as she looked for her ticket. "Oh yes, thank you, young man" she said, and no sooner had the words left her mouth when she looked up to see him zigzagging through the crowd with her parcel tucked firmly under his arm. At once, Aunt Mabel raised her hand and pointed at him and was about to shout "STOP, THIEF" when she realised that all of her problems were now solved!

THE SEQUEL

There is another story that begins where our story of Aunt Mabel finishes. It is the story of a young man who stole a 'Christmas present' from a little old lady at a ferry terminus. This story is just as interesting as the story of Aunt Mabel, for it tells the story of what that young man did next. This next chapter is what the author has conjectured as to what might have happened to the young man after he made his escape.

We don't know his real name or anything about him for that matter, but for the sake of clarity, let's call our young culprit 'Henry.'

Henry was a handsome, young, athletic and quite charming fellow. He was somewhat streetwise and opportunistic - especially when he thought he could get away with a little petty theft here and there. He had made it into quite a 'sport' for its endless propensity for excitement and adventure. It was a good adrenaline rush for what would otherwise be a boring, uneventful day for him. Henry's escapades were going to land him into more trouble than he could deal with, as we will soon see...

* * * * * * * *

Henry didn't stop running until he was two blocks away where he darted up an alley to investigate his prize more closely. He sat and waited until he got his breath back, then peeked around the corner to make sure nobody was coming, and then carefully began to unwrap the "present" without tearing the wrapping paper.

The present didn't have a label stating: "To so-and-so with love" or anything else to determine who it was for, or what was inside. But it didn't take long though before Henry had enough of the wrapper off to see that it was an electric frypan box inside. Well, Henry felt that he had just won first prize at a raffle. He carefully rewrapped the parcel and made his way home with the parcel tucked under his arm, feeling very pleased with himself.

Now each year at Henry's house there was always a big family gathering of aunts, uncles, cousins and close friends. They came from near and far. Christmas was the big event of the year that everybody looked forward to. There would be gifts, food, games, and even a game of backyard-cricket if the weather was favourable.

Although Henry was a bit of a rascal, a 'black sheep' of the family as he was often referred to by his kinfolk, he was still loved by all. Henry knew that he was loved by his family, and he thought that by giving his mother an electric frypan for Christmas might make amends for all his waywardness and for the anxieties he had caused his mother throughout the year. She was a good kind-hearted woman who tended to overlook her son's 'misdeeds' on too many an occasion.

Henry placed the gift under the Christmas tree and added a hand-drawn card with a note: "To Mum: A token of my love and appreciation towards you for all that you've done for me over the years."

Christmas Day came, and Henry couldn't wait to give his Mother his special gift. As everyone gathered excitedly around the beautifully decorated Christmas tree, Henry stood up and made quite a show of presenting her with the beautifully wrapped Christmas gift - complete with ribbon and bright red bow attached.

"To my dearest Mother." He exclaimed in a voice loud enough for all to hear.

"I hope you love this gift as much as I loved choosing it for you." and handed her the gift.

P.S. There is someone in Australia who knows the rest of this story. I don't know where to begin researching for the final outcome of this tale, but I suspect that hospital medical records might be a good place to start.

Fabrication of Events Report

As was pointed out in the preface, much of the story had to be embellished due to a lack in the author's ability to recall the details of the story. Here is a list of what was true and what was fabricated (so as to give some authenticity to the story):

Mabel was her name	False
Mabel was an aunt	Unknown.Most likely a title of endearment given to a close family friend of my Grandfather.
Mabel lived in Todmorden	False
James Walton	False
Anne Shackleton	False
Mabel had art lessons	False
Rev. Arthur Madden	False
Mabel was an artist	False
Emigrated from England	False
Suzanne a friend	False
Lived in Chatswood	False
Lived in Bankstown	False

Lived in Granville	False
Changed curtains	False
Mabel was a photographer	False
Mabel was a spinster her whole life.	Unknown marital status. She may have been a widow at the time of the events in the story.
Mabel couldn't drive	Unknown
Cat's name was Tiddles	False
Cat placed in elec. frypan carton	False. It was a hat box
Carton wrapped in Xmas paper	True
Ground hard in backyard	False
Went to Council Park	False
Took train & ferry to Manly	True
Sailors in boat	True
Young man steals carton	True
Man's name Henry	False
Zigzags through crowd	True
Man gives dead cat to Mother	False
Mabel had a cup of tea	True

The painting that was an inspiration to Aunt Mabel.

The Sunbeam Frypan

Photo Credits

Tiddles. Free images made available on the web by the Pixabay community.

Monitor SIX-20 camera. Photo used by permission - Jim Grey (USA)

Photos of Aunt Mabel, James & Anna Walton, Rev. Arthur Madden and Suzanne were all plucked from the family photo album to help guide the reader 'down the garden path.' (I do trust that you enjoyed the journey.)

True identities in order: Gwendaline, James & Harriett, William, and Amy. (Surnames have been withheld.)

Todmorden - Wikipedia encyclopedia.

https://en.wikipedia.org/wiki/Todmorden

Todmorden railway station - Roger Birch, p.24 of his book "Todmorden Album, Peoples, Places, and Events. Vol.2" used by permission.

Sydney Ferry - "Kangaroo" Courtesy of the Ross and Pat Craig Collection, University of Newcastle (Australia) now in the public domain.

Sailing Ship. Unknown artist. A print from the 1950's.

Sunbeam Frypan Ad. Woman's Weekly 1st May 1957

Cover photo by the author.

Afterword

Although the story of Aunt Mabel's dead cat is mostly fiction that was based upon a true occurrence, it wasn't until the author had finished writing the book and then sought to find a suitable design for a cover that the "true" Aunt Mabel emerged. It was with this in mind that the author has decided to add the backstory to this most interesting saga.

* * * * * * * *

After I had finished writing the book, I then sought to create the image for the front cover - a photo of an old lady holding her pet cat in period costume with 1950's furniture to set the scene, and let's not forget, I needed a black and white tabby cat to complete the "hero" front page image.

It all seemed to be fairly straight-forward in my imagination. The original pose was for "Aunt Mabel" (my wife) to be standing at a kitchen sink washing dishes with the cat sitting on the windowsill watching the proceedings attentively. So, the first thing to be found was a 1950's style house that hadn't been renovated. That wasn't as easy as was first imagined.

With fruitless searches around the town there was no success whatever, (either the kitchen had just been renovated, or the original casement windows had aluminium sliding windows fitted.) In frustration, I eventually approached the local Council for permission to use "Ringsfield House," a heritage-listed old home in nearby Nanango as a setting. A month later, after all the cogs of governance had turned through the protocols of 'due process,' permission was finally granted. By this stage my wife, Sue, had found a classy 1950's style dress that looked perfect for the occasion. Now to find a cat that fitted the description, was friendly, and wasn't riddled with fleas!

After a long and arduous search for the elusive "feline with whiskers," and having exhausted all lines of inquiry amongst friends and neighbours, things were looking rather depressing, but then - an inspiration! The local animal shelter was sure to have the odd stray cat amongst their animal domiciles, and a quick visit proved this to be the case.

The caretaker, upon hearing of my plight was happy to assist, and shewed me a number of cats that fitted the bill perfectly - all were of the black and white tabby variety, very friendly, and best of all - no fleas! All I had to do was come back the next day, borrow a cat, and proceed to Ringsfield House with my wife dressed for the photo shoot. There was only one small issue to be sorted, and that was to get approval from the animal shelter's Head Quarters located in Brisbane.

The following day, with expectations running high, I drove to the animal shelter to find that the lady at the counter was not so cheery as the day before. Upon enquiry, she exclaimed that the bosses at HQ had informed her that the xxxxx organisation was "...not in the business of lending out cats!" And with that, I put on a brave face and slowly backed away with a few parting words full of optimism - that was only betrayed by a facial expression that said otherwise.

What to do now?

It was at this stage that I realised that I needed help, Divine help, as everything within my resources had come to nothing. Months had passed from finishing the book and now I'd run into a brick wall with the cover design. I didn't want to go the way of A.I. as it was a "true story" that I was telling so I didn't want to introduce too much unreality as there was a fair dose of it in the book already. I appealed to God's assistance and left it at that.

A week or so later, I was in a town in New South Wales helping my mate Phil move house. While I was assisting him with packing up stuff in his garage, our wives went shopping for some essential items. It was there that Sue and Liz had an unexpected meeting with a good friend, Gayle Olrich, who wanted to say her good-byes for the last time before we left.

It was at the end of the conversation that Gayle commented that she had to get home to feed her tabby cat.

"A tabby cat!" both exclaimed. "What colour is it?" ... and the rest is now history. Gayle lived in the same street as our friends and was only too happy to have her "Puddy" feature on the cover of a new book.

The photo shoot with my wife dressed up and the cat on her lap was *not* a success. The cat wasn't happy and nor was Sue. There was definitely no "chemistry" in their relationship. Puddy's ears poked straight-out sideways. Cranky but tolerant would best describe the cat's mood. It was at the end of a gruelling half-hour that Gayle suggested that she could take on the part of Aunt Mabel tomorrow and hope for better success. And this we did.

It was during one of these times that Gayle began to tell us the history of her cat Puddy.

AFTERWORD

Just like in the story:-

1. "Puddy" was also a stray that was adopted by a lady.

2. Both kittens had wandered into a house yard.

3. Dorothy Franks, the original owner of Puddy, came from Farnworth, an English town about 30km from Todmordon, where Aunt Mabel was born.

4. The kitten was originally called "Toodles" by Dorothy's daughter, Gina, who was just a child at the time.

5. Dorothy gave the cat to Gayle Olrich when she wasn't able to care for it any longer. It was Dorothy who called the cat "Puddy."

6. As in the book, Gayle and Puddy were just like Aunt Mable and Tiddles, in that their cats were more than just pets. They were their special home companions.

7. And of course, both Tiddles and Puddy were black and white tabby cats.

Sadly, Puddy died at the full age of eighteen years old in January 2025.

In memory of Puddy

Epilogue

It has come as a surprise to some that the Certificate of Excellence award shown on the cover of this book was an *actual award* given by the Cat Writers' (CWA) in America for the first edition of this book.

The award was given for the best book entered into the "Entertainment" category for this year's annual competition (2025).

There were over thirty categories that authors from around the world could send their literary works to the CWA for judging of their books on its merits.

It is with the utmost appreciation and gratitude that the author is delighted to have received such an award from the CWA. The organisation is run mostly by volunteers who have a passion about the care and welfare of cats.

For further information about the Cat Writers' Association: https://catwriters.com/

www.ingramcontent.com/pod-product-compliance
Lightning Source LLC
Chambersburg PA
CBHW042034120726
47911CB00027B/742

* 9 7 8 0 6 4 5 7 3 7 1 7 2 *